Canals

Written by Ratu Mataira

Rigby

Canals are made so boats can go from place to place.

Some canals are so small that big boats cannot go in them.

3

Some canals are very big.
They are so big that big ships can go in them.

This big canal is in the desert.

5

Some canals are made so boats can go up and down hills. These canals have locks.

The locks have gates.

gates

locks

How a Lock Works:

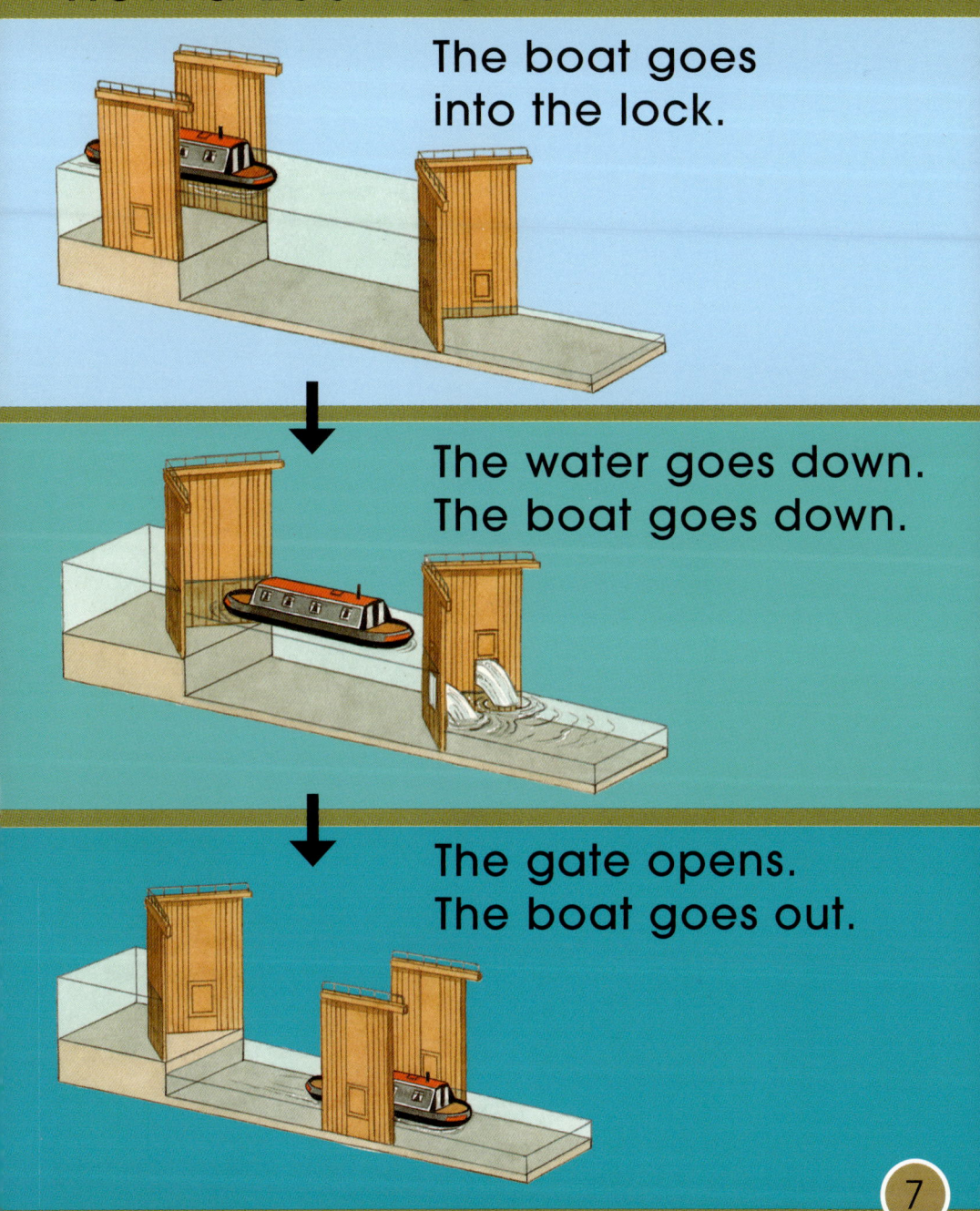

The boat goes into the lock.

The water goes down.
The boat goes down.

The gate opens.
The boat goes out.

Locks can help
boats go
around places.

This boat is going
around a waterfall.

Some locks are so big
that very big ships
can go in and out
of them.

waterfall

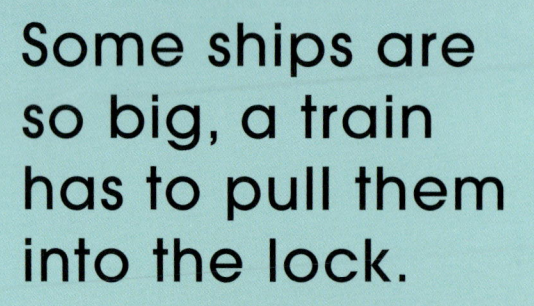

Some ships are so big, a train has to pull them into the lock.

train

11

On some canals,
boats can go
up and down hills.
But they don't go
in a lock.
They go in a boat lift.

Some boat lifts
look like
big swimming pools.

The boat lift goes up
and down the hill.
It takes boats
from one canal
to the other.

tracks

canal

boat lift

13

This is a very big boat lift.
It can take boats from
one canal to the other, too.
But it goes around and around!

1. The boat goes into the boat lift.

2. The boat lift goes around.

14

Index

canals for big boats
. . . . 4, 8, 10

canals for small boats
. . . . 2

how boat lifts work
. . . . 12, 14

how locks work
. . . . 6-8

why canals are made
. . . . 2, 6

The boat goes out of the boat lift.

Guide Notes

Title: Canals
Stage: Early (3) – Blue

Genre: Nonfiction
Approach: Guided Reading
Processes: Thinking Critically, Exploring Language, Processing Information
Written and Visual Focus: Photographs (static images), Index, Labels, Caption, Flow Diagram

THINKING CRITICALLY
(sample questions)
- Look at the front cover and the title. Ask the children what they know about canals.
- Look at the title and read it to the children.
- Focus the children's attention on the index. Ask: "What are you going to find out about in this book?"
- If you want to find out why canals are made, what pages would you look on?
- If you want to find out how a boat lift works, what pages would you look on?
- Look at pages 2 and 3. How do you think these canals might have been made?
- Look at pages 10 and 11. How else do you think the big ships could be helped into a lock?

EXPLORING LANGUAGE

Terminology
Title, cover, photographs, author, photographers

Vocabulary
Interest words: canal, lock, desert, ship, gates, waterfall
High-frequency words: so, other, around
Positional words: around, out, into, up, down, in, on
Compound words: cannot, into, waterfall

Print Conventions
Capital letter for sentence beginnings, periods, commas, exclamation mark